THE GECKO
AND THE ECHO

For Ziggy, who taught me that paradise is wherever you choose to see it. Thank you for the rainbows – R B

In memory of Doogy, who liked a party – J F

ORCHARD BOOKS

First published in Great Britain in 2022 by Hodder & Stoughton
First published in paperback in 2023

1 3 5 7 9 10 8 6 4 2

Text © Rachel Bright, 2022
Illustrations © Jim Field, 2022

The moral rights of the author and illustrator have been asserted.

A CIP catalogue record for this book is available from the British Library.

HB 978 1 40835 606 7
PB 978 1 40835 607 4

Printed and bound in China

FSC
www.fsc.org
MIX
Paper from
responsible sources
FSC® C104740

Orchard Books, an imprint of Hachette Children's Group
Part of Hodder & Stoughton
Carmelite House,
50 Victoria Embankment,
London EC4Y 0DZ
An Hachette UK Company
www.hachette.co.uk
www.hachettechildrens.co.uk

Rachel
BRIGHT

Jim
FIELD

THE GECKO
AND THE ECHO

ORCHARD

On a tropical island that rose from the seas,
Where the welcome was warm on the coconut breeze,
One little gecko: flamboyant, expressive . . .
Felt quite unique and *extremely* impressive!

"I am Goldy the Great!
Check me out! Drink it in!
Hear me sing! Watch me
dance! I can do *anything!*
Some day very soon
I will be a GREAT STAR.
I KNOW if I practise
that I will go far!"

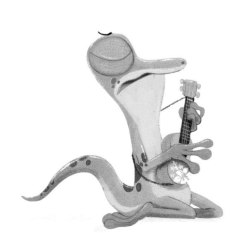

So Goldy would prance
and play to the crowd,
Singing songs out of tune
and *incredibly* loud!

It was 24/7! That mouth never shut!
Yes, Goldy was frankly . . .

... A PAIN IN THE BUTT!

At breakfast, guess who would be first to the mango, FANDANGLING them all with a pushing-in tango?!

At nap time, young Goldy would sashay and croon,

Waking the tiniest geckos TOO SOON!

And under the moon,
when the whole bay would dance,
There'd be hops to the front
at every chance!

Day in and night out,
Goldy just wouldn't stop,
With no care where to tread
on the way to the TOP.

Then, one fateful night when the crickets were chirping,
Goldy tried making a tune . . . out of *burping!*

RRRRPPP!

The others decided this was the LAST STRAW – They just couldn't take Goldy's gifts any more!

"ENOUGH!" they implored.
"You're all *ME! ME! ME!*
We don't want to listen!
It's **TOO MUCH**, don't you see?!"

Goldy was shocked!
Dumbfounded and stunned!
Greatness like this should **NEVER** be shunned!
They were just the wrong audience —
that was a fact.
It was time to go elsewhere
to practise this act!

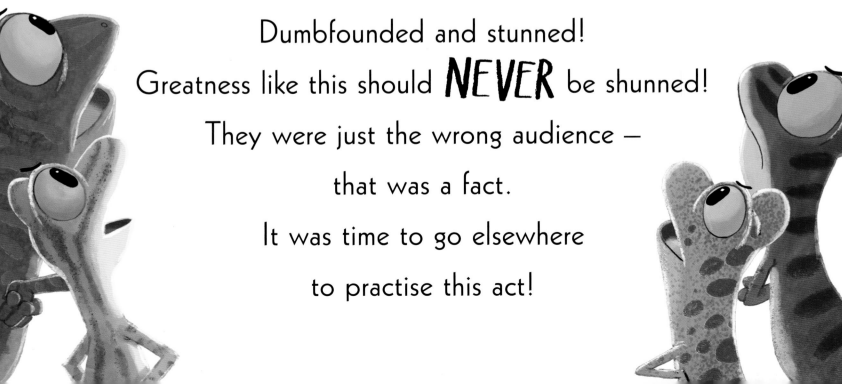

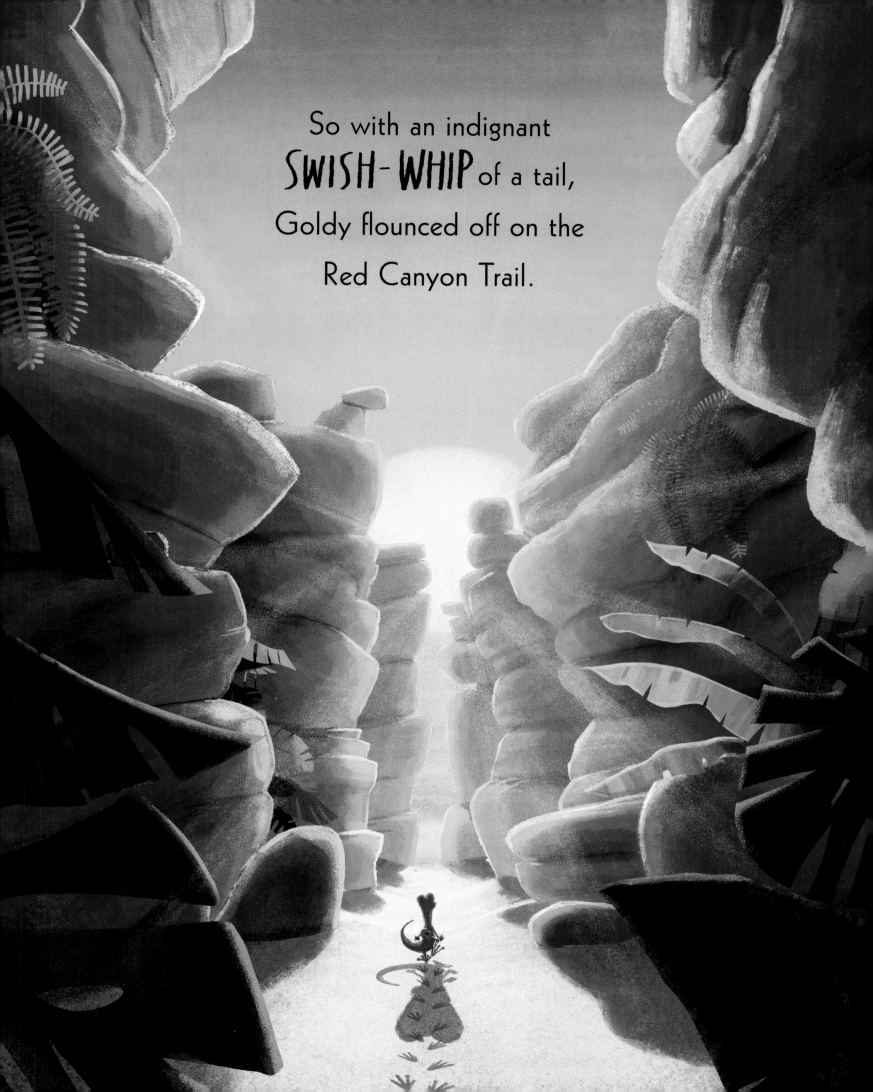

So with an indignant
SWISH-WHIP of a tail,
Goldy flounced off on the
Red Canyon Trail.

In the empty crevasse, a voice could **RING** out,
BELT out a tune . . . free a burp . . . have a shout!

With a smile and a jump, Goldy let out a, "WOOOOOOOO!"
But before the next, "HOOOO..."

. . . came another voice too!

"WOOOOOOOOOOOOOOOOOOOOOOOOOO!"

But no one was there! So, who'd **WOOO-D** on the **HOOO**?! There just wasn't room on this rock-stage for two.

Goldy tried singing a

" **TRA-LA-LA-LA...** "

But got *drowned out* by singing that bounced . . . twice as far!

" **TRALALALA LALALAAAA!** "

And the song was *not* good! It was all out of tune!
Who? Goldy thought, *is this other* BUFFOON?!

"BE QUIET!" Goldy hollered.

" BE QUIETTTTTT!" came the shout.

This other gecko would have to GET OUT!

But then ever so quietly,

across the blue sky

some SURPRISE INSPIRATION

came fluttering by . . . .

"Hello there," it tinkled.

"I have an idea . . . . "

Whispering gently in young

Goldy's ear . . . .

"The voice that you hear . . . it isn't a gecko.
That shouting and singing . . . it's simply an ECHO."

"WHAT?!" spluttered Goldy.
"That can't possibly be!
That terrible wailing? That ruckus
was . . .

ME?"

Well . . . Goldy was stumped.
Could this really be true?
If it was, then this KNOWING
was urgent and new.

The koa said, "Greatness —
it's not **WHAT** you do,
But **HOW** you are doing it
. . . *that* matters too!"

Goldy felt *changed*,
"A new day is dawning!
I **MUST** hurry back to
my family this morning.

I want to return
to my sparkling bay
And perform in a new,
VERY different way!"

So at breakfast time *now* Goldy says, "After you . . . "
With a slow-waltz-reverse to the back of the queue!

When babies get tired
and are closing their eyes,

Goldy hums soft, snoozy,
hushed lullabies.

And under the moon
when they gather at night,
Goldy just can't help but
groove in the limelight . . . **BUT** . . .

. . . *now* those manoeuvres
are mindful and kind —
For all those in front
AND all those behind . . .

. . . Uniting *all* geckos to **DANCE** and to **SING**,
Making **THEM** feel they could do *anything*.
This was *real* **STARDOM!** Who would've thought?!
With fan clubs and fame of a *much* better sort . . .

Yes, Goldy found out what
TRUE GREATNESS can be,
Not just for one, but for you and for me.
Whatever our journey, whichever our track,
What we send out will come echoing back.

And so, if we know that we
GET what we GIVE . . .

. . . then giving out

LOVE

is a great

way to live.